To my friend Kuldip and all the other girls
who dream of exploring the stars

Text and illustrations copyright © Ken Wilson Max 2019
First published in Great Britain in 2019 by Otter-Barry Books,
Little Orchard, Burley Gate, Herefordshire, HR1 3QS
www.otterbarrybooks.com

A catalogue record for this book is available from the British Library.
ISBN 978-1-910959-21-3

Illustrated with acrylic paint
Set in Hand Drawn Shapes

Printed in China

9 8 7 6 5 4 3 2

ASTRO GIRL

Ken Wilson-Max

Otter-Barry BOOKS

Astrid had loved the stars and space ever since she could remember.

"I want to be an astronaut," Astrid told her best friend Jake as they gazed up at the stars.

"Will you bring me an asteroid when you come back from space?" asked Jake.

"Of course I will, Jakey."

"I want to be an astronaut!"
Astrid said at breakfast.

"Are you sure?" Papa asked. "You'll have to go round and round the Earth in your spaceship."

He swung her around.

"I can do that," Astrid giggled.

"I can do that," said Astrid, munching a cereal bar.

"OK, Astro Girl,
you'll also have to get
used to near-zero gravity...."
Papa threw her up in the air.

"I can do that all day long," laughed Astrid.

"What about all the science experiments?" asked Papa. "Could you do those, my star princess?"

"Easy-peasy!" said Astrid, as they made her favourite cookies.

"Will a **space cadet** like you be able to **sleep** on your **own** among the **stars**?" Papa asked.

"I think that will be very hard... but I'll do it!" Astrid whispered.

At last it was the day they were going to fetch
Mama in the car. Astrid wore her favourite space
T-shirt.

At the airbase, they moved to the front of the crowd just in time for the doors to open.

Out walked three people.

"Mama!" shouted Astrid.
They hugged and she gave her mum a big kiss.

"Mama, I missed you!

I want to be an astronaut, just like you. You're my hero."

This is what Astrid found when she read all the books she could find about being an astronaut....

The word 'astronaut' comes from two Greek words: *Astron* meaning *star* and *Nautes* meaning *sailor.*

American astronauts Neil Armstrong and Buzz Aldrin were the first to land on the moon, in the lunar module 'Eagle', on 20th July, 1969.

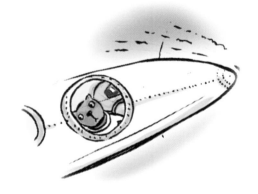

The first animal to go into orbit was Laika the dog, on board the Soviet Sputnik 2 spacecraft on 3rd November, 1957.

Valentina Tereshkova, from Russia, was the first woman in space, in **1963**.

Shannon Matilda Wells Lucid, from the USA, set the record for the longest time spent in space by a woman. (**188** days in **1966**)

Mae Carol Jemison was the first African American woman in space, in **1992**.

Helen Sharman was the first British astronaut and the first woman to visit the Mir Space station, in **1991**.

Kalpana Chawla was the first woman of Indian origin in space, in **1997**.

Space food is dried so that it will not spill or leak and cause any damage to machines. Fruit, bread and nuts are OK as they are.

Astronauts train underwater to create the feeling of floating in space.